The Little Giraffe

Retold by Lesley Sims

Illustrated by Laure Fournier

Reading Consultant: Alison Kelly
Roehampton University

Once, there was
a little giraffe.

He was the first
giraffe in the world.

He lived in
East Africa...

...with his
best friend,
Rhino.

5

Every day, they looked
for food.

But the sun was hot

and the earth was dry.

8

There was no
food anywhere.

9

So they went to see...

"Come back tomorrow," said the wise man.

"I'll make a magic drink for you."

The next day, the
little giraffe visited
the wise man.

"Here's the drink!" he said. "Where's Rhino?"

The little giraffe didn't know.

The little giraffe began
to drink.

He grew taller...

and
taller...

"Now you can reach the
leaves high in the trees,"
said the wise man.

Rhino had found
some dry grass.

He forgot all about
the wise man.

"There you are," said the not-so-little giraffe.

What happened to you?

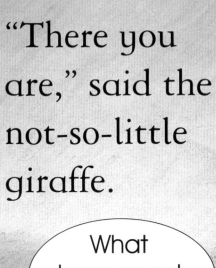

"I drank the magic drink," he said to Rhino.

Where's mine?

There was no magic drink left.

Rhino was stuck
with dry grass.

He was
angry with
the giraffe and
the wise man.

And he was angry
with himself.

He's still angry today.

Puzzles

Puzzle 1

Can you spot eight differences between these two pictures?

Puzzle 2

Put the six pictures in order.

A

B

C

D

E

F

Puzzle 3
Find these things
in the picture:

huts
trees
Rhino
little giraffe
birds
footprints

Puzzle 4
Choose the best sentence
in each picture.

He's angry.   He's happy.

29

Answers to puzzles

Puzzle 1

Puzzle 2

E C B

F A D

Puzzle 3

birds
trees
huts
Rhino
little giraffe
footprints

Puzzle 4

"It's hot."   "I'm tall."   He's angry.

The Little Giraffe is a folktale
from East Africa.

Designed by Samantha Meredith

First published in 2007 by Usborne Publishing Ltd., Usborne House,
83-85 Saffron Hill, London EC1N 8RT, England. www.usborne.com
Copyright © 2007 Usborne Publishing Ltd.